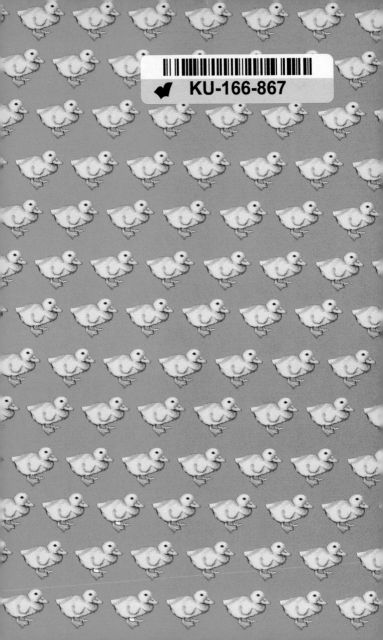

KU-166-867

Published by Ladybird Books Ltd
Penguin Books Ltd, 80 Strand, London WC2R 0RL, England
Penguin (Group) Australia, 250 Camberwell Road, Camberwell, Victoria 3124, Australia
Penguin Group (NZ), cnr Airborne and Rosedale Roads, Albany, Auckland 1310,
New Zealand
A Penguin Company

1 3 5 7 9 10 8 6 4 2
This presentation copyright © Ladybird Books Ltd, 2006
New reproductions of Beatrix Potter's book illustrations copyright © Frederick Warne & Co.,
2002
Original text and illustrations copyright © Frederick Warne & Co., 1908

Additional illustrations by Colin Twinn and Alex Vining

ISBN-13: 978-1-8464-6355-6
ISBN-10: 1-8464-6355-6

Printed in Italy

THE TALE OF
JEMIMA PUDDLE-DUCK

A SIMPLIFIED RETELLING OF THE ORIGINAL TALE BY
BEATRIX POTTER

This is the story of Jemima
Puddle-duck.

Jemima lived on a farm.
She wanted to hatch her own
eggs but the farmer's wife
would not let her.

Jemima's sister, Rebeccah, did not want to hatch her own eggs.

"I would not look after them properly, and neither would you, Jemima," said Rebeccah.

Jemima tried to hide her
eggs so that she could look
after them.

But Jemima's eggs were always
taken away from her.

One day Jemima left the farm
so she could lay her eggs.

She wore a blue bonnet and a
pink shawl.

Jemima Puddle-duck ran
down the hill and then
jumped off into the air.

She flew over the tree-tops
looking for a place to land.

 12

Jemima landed in the wood and saw someone reading a newspaper.

"Quack?" said Jemima.

The gentleman looked at
Jemima. "Have you lost
your way?" he said.

Jemima told the gentleman
that she was trying to find
a place to lay her eggs.

The gentleman said,
"I have a shed. You may lay
your eggs in there."

He opened the door and
let Jemima in.

The shed was full of feathers.
It was very comfortable
and soft. Jemima Puddle-duck
made a nest.

She laid nine eggs.

The next day, the gentleman
said to Jemima, "Let us have
a dinner party."

"Bring some herbs from the farm and I will make an omelette."

Jemima met Kep.
He knew those herbs were
for cooking roast duck!

Kep ran to the village and told the puppies.

Jemima went back to
the wood and found
the gentleman.

He spoke in an angry voice. "Check your eggs and then come into my house. Quickly!"

Jemima felt afraid.

Kep and the puppies found
the shed in the wood. They
shut Jemima in the shed to
keep her safe.

Then they chased the
gentleman away.
He never came back.

Kep opened the door of
the shed and let Jemima
Puddle-duck out.

Then Kep and the puppies
took Jemima back to the farm.

Jemima laid some more eggs and she was allowed to hatch them herself. She had four yellow ducklings.

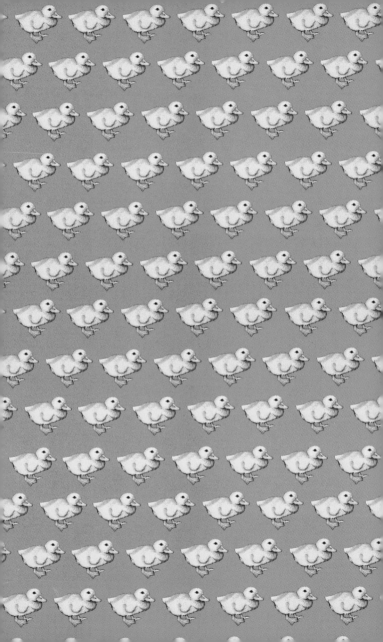